W9-AUT-653

The President's Puppy

by Linda Oatman High
Illustrated by Steve Björkman

Hello Reader! — Level 4

SCHOLASTIC INC.
Cartwheel
B·O·O·K·S ®

New York   Toronto   London   Auckland   Sydney
Mexico City   New Delhi   Hong Kong   Buenos Aires

Fido was a yellow dog.

He was the color of golden honey.

Fido's ears were long and droopy.

His fur was thick.

Fido's gentle, brown eyes smiled.

His tail waved like a flag.

His home was in the small town
of Springfield, Illinois.
Fido lived with the Lincoln family:
Abraham and Mary, and their sons
named Willie and Tad.

Fido walked with Abe Lincoln every morning.
They walked to the market.
Fido proudly held a brown bundle in his mouth
as they strolled home.
People stopped to pet Fido.
They talked about how he was a good dog.
Everybody in the town knew Fido.

Fido went with Abe Lincoln
to Billy the Barber's.
Fido waited patiently on the porch while Abe had
his hair cut.
Fido thumped his tail when Abe returned.

Fido went with Abe Lincoln and his sons to
Diller's Drugstore.
He shared fruit-flavored soda water with
Willie and Tad.

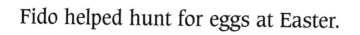

Fido helped hunt for eggs at Easter.

In the summer, Fido went swimming
while Willie fished.

Fido liked to play in piles of leaves in the fall.

Fido ate turkey at Thanksgiving.

He received gifts at Christmas.

And he went sledding with Tad when it snowed.

Fido loved to run in circles after his tail.
He loved to roll on the floor with Abe Lincoln
and the boys.
Fido loved to have his floppy ears scratched.

And Fido loved to sit in the kitchen
when Mary Lincoln was cooking.
She gave him tastes of food.

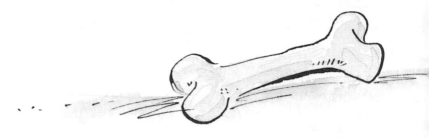

Fido's favorite trick was fetching sticks.
Fido liked playing ball, too.

Fido led a carefree life until
the year of 1860.
That was when Abe Lincoln
was elected president of the United States.
Then Fido's whole life changed.

Loud cannons exploded.

Church bells rang all over town.

People were celebrating. They pushed their way
into the Lincolns' home, cheering.

They squeezed into the parlor where Fido
was trying to sleep. People tripped over Fido.
They kicked him by accident.

Fido was scared. He shook and moaned.
Fido crawled beneath the old horsehair sofa.
He hid from the crowds.
He wished they would leave. Fido wanted
to have his family all to himself.

The next morning, Fido trotted behind
Abe Lincoln to the market.
Fido thought it would be like every
other morning.
But everyone wanted Abe Lincoln to stop and talk.
Fido sighed. Nobody petted him.
Nobody said that he was a good dog.

Abe Lincoln was so busy, he forgot to give Fido
a package to carry home from the market.
There was no time to stop at Billy the Barber's.
There was no time for soda water at
Diller's Drugstore.

There was no time to roll on the floor at home.
Abe Lincoln was too busy to throw a stick or a
ball. Fido chased his tail alone.

Then Abe Lincoln gave his sons
some sad news:
It would be best for Fido not to come to
Washington, D.C., with them.
Fido didn't like crowds. He didn't like noise.
Fido was not meant for city life.
He wouldn't like the White House.
He liked the small town of Springfield.
It was Fido's home.
He'd lived there all his life.
Fido was happy there.

Willie and Tad hung their heads.
Mary Lincoln cried. So did Abe.
Fido's eyes didn't smile. His tail didn't wag.
Fido lay on the old horsehair sofa with his
head on his paws.

Abe Lincoln thought a lot about what
would make a good home for Fido.
He considered Billy the Barber's.
He considered Diller's Drugstore.
He thought about the market.

But finally Abe Lincoln decided that Fido
would be happiest with the neighbors.
The neighbors had two young sons named
Frank and John Roll.
The boys liked Fido. They played ball
with Fido.
They threw sticks for him to fetch.
They rolled on the floor with him.

Frank and John promised to be good to Fido.
They were happy to care for him.
They would feed him special treats.
He would be part of their family.
They would love him.
The Lincolns would not have to worry.
Fido would be happy.

The Lincolns wanted to have a
photograph of Fido.
They gave Fido a bath.
They brushed him to make his fur shine.
And then they took him to a
photography studio.

Fido lay on a soft blanket. He looked
serious and proud.
Willie and Tad tried to make him smile.
Fido's picture was taken.
The Lincoln family liked the picture.
They planned to take it to Washington, D.C.,
so that they would never forget Fido.

The Lincoln family took Fido to
Diller's Drugstore.
They shared sodas. Fido had ice cream.
He licked the sticky hands of the Lincoln boys.

They went home.
Abe Lincoln played one last
game of ball with Fido.
He threw a stick for Fido to fetch.
Then he clipped a piece of Fido's fur.
He put the yellow fur in his pocket.
He would keep it forever.

The Lincoln family packed for the train trip.
Soon it was time for them to leave.
They were going to live in the White House.
The train would take them to the big city of
Washington, D.C.
Tad and Willie hugged Fido.
Mary Lincoln hugged Fido.
Abe Lincoln hugged Fido good-bye.
He kissed him. Abe had tears in his eyes.
"We'll be back," Abe said. "Always be a good dog."
Fido licked Abe Lincoln's hand. He wagged his tail.
His eyes tried to smile.

Fido dreamed of the Lincolns that night.
He slept on the old sofa.
The Lincolns dreamed of Fido.
They slept on the train.

The neighbors were nice to Fido.
Fido walked to the market with
Frank and John.
They took him to Diller's Drugstore.
He waited outside Billy the Barber's
when Frank and John went for haircuts.

Fido was happy. Springfield, Illinois was his home.
There people petted him. They talked about what a
good dog he was.
Everybody in Springfield knew Fido.

Sometimes letters came from the Lincoln family. Fido sniffed the letters. He remembered the Lincolns.

The Lincolns remembered Fido, too.
They looked at his picture.
They talked about how two families
loved him now.
Fido had lots of love.

One day, the Rolls took Fido to his old home.
But Abe Lincoln wasn't there.
Black cloth was draped everywhere.
Many strangers crowded into the house.
People were sad. They cried.
President Abraham Lincoln had died.

Fido rolled on the floor. He chased his tail.
He smiled at the people. Everybody talked about
what a great president Abe Lincoln had been. They
said that they'd remember Abe Lincoln forever.
They talked about how Fido was a good dog.
Fido looked out the window.
He saw Abe Lincoln's horse, Old Bob.
Old Bob hung his head. He looked sad.

Fido was taken back to the studio for
another photograph.
It was sold all over the United States of America.
Fido was famous.
Everybody in the country knew Fido.
But Fido was still the same old yellow dog.
He still had droopy ears. He still had thick fur.
He still loved to roll on the floor and chase his tail.
He would always be Abe Lincoln's dog.